The Mere Weight of Words

The Mere Weight of Words

a novella by Carissa Halston

Aqueous Books
New Orleans

Published by Aqueous Books
P.O. Box 6816
New Orleans, LA 70174
www.aqueousbooks.com

Published in the United States of America
ISBN: 978-0-9847399-5-0
First edition, Aqueous Books printing, June 2012
Book design and layout: Cynthia Reeser
Cover art: Randolph Pfaff

For Carolina Barerra-Tobón and Neal Bruss, two linguists kind enough to share their knowledge with others

"The term *language family* is sometimes criticized as a dangerous metaphor, suggesting as it does a biological analogy. This criticism has some justification; languages are not discrete entities, like kittens, born at one specific time and dying at another. They are not separate creatures from their 'parents;' rather, they *are* their parents."

—C.M. Millward, *The Biography of the English Language*

I. Predicament

I learn of my father's condition online. While reading the Arts and Leisure section of the *Times*, I see a thumbnail-sized photo of him appear in the sidebar:

Notable Filmmaker Suffers from Alzheimer's Disease

I stop breathing on the exhale. My lips and eyes grow arid before I breathe again. I know the initial shock has worn off when I start considering the semantics and pragmatics of the headline. I can hear his dander rising and standing erect. He invades my internal monologue.

"Notable? *Notable?* I've been nominated for three Academy Awards!" But he's never won. "My most recent picture screened at Cannes!" A city whose name the average American filmgoer cannot properly pronounce. "My films were *saying something* while their movies were pandering *trash*. The gall. 'Notable!'"

I thought the term fit perfectly. Notable. Not. Able.

That's not a reflection of his work—I've always enjoyed his films, particularly when he hasn't—but more a judgment of his ability to properly function as a normal being in society. He hasn't been famous his entire life—he hasn't even been famous for my entire life—but once he achieved that initial modicum of celebrity, it was as if he'd arrived in the echelons where he always assumed he had every right to be. Perhaps that's why I fault him for his behavior: I remember what he was like before his notoriety.

I ponder the concept of his withering memories, his recollections, once solid and distinct, becoming wispy and insubstantial, eventually melting into nothingness. Having never been what most would consider an attractive man, it's been said that my father's greatest gift is his mind. "How must he be taking that?" my thoughts idle. I stumble past a feeling that might be pity, but it emits an unmistakable bitterness even as I stagger to avoid it. I soon clench a similar, yet wholly separate sense, like guilt commingled with nausea. An idiom about apple trees and the fruit they bear flits through my mind and I'm buffered by a strange solace: even from afar, no one knows him better than I do.

My father's work is destined to be remembered and reviewed by his fans, critics, and contemporaries, but his personal life has only ever been visible to a select few: my mother, myself, and my father's closest friend, Eliot, a long-time executive at the film studio that released his first major motion picture.

It's Eliot who calls me, months after I'm made aware of my father's illness.

"Meredith?" he ventures, guessing he got the right number, who knows how.

"Yes, who is this?" I answer warily, worried that my number has been made known to telemarketers, the sort who coyly drop last names in an effort to ensnare the aged, the bored, and the feeble-minded.

"Hi—this is Eliot Langren." My mouth creases shut, lips flattening in a sure effort to keep me from talking. "I hope you remember me." I consider hanging up. "I'm a friend of your father's."

"Hello Eliot," my voice barely emerges from my mouth. My scar makes it difficult to speak sometimes, but this specific bout of paralysis emanates from nerve damage of a different sort.

"Meredith, I'm calling for your Dad."

"I know."

"Oh," his voice spells relief. "Then you already know about his situation."

"What does he want?" I lack the constitution to waste time with euphemisms.

"He, ah—" Eliot's reticence speaks volumes.

"Jesus. He doesn't know you're calling me."

"No," he admits. "No, he doesn't. He wouldn't ask for help."

"Help." The word is a half-hearted question, but surfaces more as an accusation.

"He needs you," Eliot tells me.

"I find that hard to believe."

"Everyone needs their family." I want this to be an ironic gesture, but Eliot isn't the type who goes in for irony. Every ounce of his plea stands in earnest.

"There's nothing I can do," I say dismissively, then hang up. I experience a passing desire to call back and apologize, but lack the nerve. It isn't a conversation I'm prepared to have.

Eliot calls again the following morning. I recognize the number.

"You're diligent, Eliot."

"I wouldn't bother you if it wasn't important," he says.

"I just don't see how I could make any difference. He's not *dying*," I tell him. "Not in a way that a transfusion or kidney or marrow would help."

"In a way, it's worse," Eliot says.

A terse puff of air escapes between my tightly slackened teeth. "What do you expect from me? What could I possibly do?"

"Talk to him," Eliot urges me.

"What, on the phone?"

"God, no. He's awful on the phone."

"I remember."

Eliot pauses, likely in the hopes that such piddling nostalgia will bring me around. "Will you go see him?"

Although Eliot can't see me, I throw up my hands in his general direction. "What other choice do I have? You'll just keep calling me and I'm too proud to change my number or block yours."

"You got that from him," Eliot says.

"I got too much." Before he can counter, I tell him to mail me the particulars of the meeting. "I want something in writing."

"In writing?" he repeats.

"Don't worry, I'm not going to the press with anything," I promise. "I just want to see the words." I listen to Eliot's breath as he considers this.

"Okay," he acquiesces.

I give him my address, he repeats it back to me, and the conversation ends.

I talk to myself when the letter arrives. "I can do this. This is not bigger than I am." I delve deeper before the three-hour drive to my father's house. It's a pep talk of sorts. "Best case scenario: neither of you will say anything, and then you'll get to go home that much sooner. Worst case scenario: he'll incense you into a foaming rage and then die on the spot, forever cementing your estrangement and guilting you in the process." I take a deep breath as I pull out of my driveway. "You can't spell *estrangement* without *strange*."

*

It's been almost two decades since I last spoke to my father. In addition to larger obstacles, I blame him for little things: my crooked teeth, my poor posture, physical manifestations of a hereditary sort, easily viewed by a third party and thus, rational points of contention. But the main reasons behind our damaged relationship are more difficult to prove. On my way to his house, I enumerate and categorize as much as I can recall.

The minor quibbles are easy to discount as an amalgamation of our collective stubborn tendencies: it's simultaneously both and neither of our faults. We fought like alley cats, lashing out in order to exact our territory. For a time, we mended fences like cats as well. We'd lick each other's wounds, try to apologize, but it sometimes exacerbated things, leading to redoubled efforts, the verbal equivalent of swatting, biting, and leaping at each other with exposed claws.

This type of recollection makes our disagreements seem

trivial. And perhaps they are. But when I weighed them with my apprentice heart, gauged them by my protégé pride, and fretted over them with an almost spousal concern, I found them—and, on some days, still find them—the most important moments in my life. They laid the foundation of the person I would become. While I have since changed, they affected who I am today by determining who I never could be.

Every small argument we waged underlined the two major qualms I have with my father: his shoddy treatment of my mother and his overbearing expectations regarding my career. The former, which albeit had little to do with me, nettled me nonetheless. I was young and had chosen sides, placed blame, held grudges. But even if I had been older, it was difficult not to return with a verdict against him. Look at the words we use: *cheat*, *guilt*, *lie*, *judge*. Strong, monosyllabic, weighty terms that allow us to distance ourselves from a situation we're not properly trained to assess.

In the years since, the answers to difficult questions seem more obvious. Were there other women? Of course. How many? The number is irrelevant. No final tally hurts as much as the initial acknowledgment of betrayal. Did that mean he didn't love my mother? No, but it compromised that love and, in the process, devalued it. Could they have survived it under different circumstances? Perhaps. My presence surely complicated matters but, save an act of filicide, there was no risk of my being removed from the situation. That didn't stop me from wondering how my parents would have fared had they kept a childless marriage.

Guilt runs deeply through my veins, especially the self-inflicted sort.

I am rankled over my inability to remember a single turning point that soured my father in my mind. No individual instance stands out as worse than the others. No monumental signal (like forgetting to thank my mother at an award ceremony or spending too much time with a single leading lady) outshines the collective slights he paid us. Our differences might have been overcome if there had been one moment. One distinct act could have been explained away—too much stress, not enough support, a temper emerging at an inopportune time. But the gradual descent, the mire we each marched through, became insurmountable.

Not long after the divorce was final, I asked my mother when she fell out of love with my father. It seemed a less overwrought question than, "When did you realize your marriage was over?" Her answer surprised me.

"We were on the train." That meant in New York. "And a man got up to offer his seat to me."

"That's it?" I asked when she didn't continue. "What happened?"

"Nothing. Your father didn't bat an eye, didn't thank the man, didn't say a word. He failed to recognize the gesture's gravity." Failed. Gravity. Her words said it all. "Though, really, that's not surprising. For all his insight, your father has never noticed that sort of kindness in anyone. Such facets just don't resonate with him."

"But they resonate with you."

She nodded. "That small act nearly moved me to tears. It had been so long since I'd thought of myself as worthy of notice. And even longer since I wondered why your father didn't."

"Did you say anything to him?"

"What could I have said?" she asked. "Even if I had said something, he would have accused me of overreacting. Or of being needy."

"Having too thin skin..."

"Something like that." She let out a perfunctory sigh. "We were divorced within a year."

"He didn't ask why?"

"I'm not sure it mattered to him. I asked for it; he complied. For him, I'm sure it was a form of wish fulfillment. He was simply granting my request."

"How generous," I bristled.

"Try not to hold it against him. He did the best he could."

Conversations such as this convince me that my willingness to hold a grudge stems from a paternal gene, so boundless is my mother's selflessness.

Conversely, the other major grievance I hold against my

father involves some selfishness on my part. In my young adulthood, most of the conversations we had centered on my future plans and I was foolish enough to think I had a choice in the matter. My desires notwithstanding, these disputes were largely one-sided. When he wanted to, my father communicated with an ease of manner that I've not seen in anyone since. His command of the spoken language could have made him a politician or an orator, if people still aspired to be things such as orators. As a linguist, I find his command of speech fascinating. As his daughter, I find it nerve-racking, intimidating, and unfair, though I had to work up to that level of scorn. Having never been particularly chatty, I spent a great deal of my childhood in awe of my father's eloquence. However, upon reaching teenage reticence, my admiration became envy. I harbored feverish hopes that his lingual gifts lay dormant in my genes and would someday blossom. I even dared to dream that I might be allowed to someday surpass him in that regard. I hold out hope even now. My father, disregarding any goals I held for my own future, wanted me to take up fine art. However, I preferred to do nothing. Or everything. Or both. I refused to make a decision.

"You need to choose," he would tell me. "I did and look where it got me."

"I'm not you," I moped. "Besides, you never have to choose. You already have everything."

"And don't you also have everything? Haven't I given you that?" he pressed.

"I didn't ask for it."

"Life can be so difficult, can't it?" He smiled at me, the smug snake, before his disgust surfaced. "I afford you the time and means to create and what do you do? You squander it. A fine batch of talent—wasted. If you were older, you'd see that."

After this, he'd usually walk around the house, repeating himself as though I couldn't hear: "Wasteful. What a waste." As if he suffered from short-term memory loss. Or maybe he felt his words gained meaning upon second or third visitation.

Since we only spoke to each other when his schedule allowed, this was almost every conversation my father and I had for over three years. Any other interaction we shared involved my schooling, though he never paid my marks more than a passing glance.

"Mm-hmm," he'd say whenever I interrupted his work to report my grades. There was never an opportune time to stop him. A cavalcade of scripts to be edited, calls to be taken, and projects to be borne of his utmost concentration persistently marched through our lives. Oddly enough, I didn't expect less than that; it wasn't his occupation or even his indifference that warranted my ire, so much as his resurgence during bouts of inactivity. Had I been otherwise left alone, I likely would have been happy to see him between three-month editing binges and last-minute meetings. He only earned my resentment by spending all our remaining free time pushing me. He pushed me in ways that he wouldn't push himself. His critiques of my artwork—my *art*work, there's a misnomer for the ages—would emerge unbidden. It was as if he desired nothing more than to remove the joy of the process for me.

"Your shading is too light," he once said while I sketched.

"It's called *value*, not shading."

"The name doesn't change the fact that it's too light. And isn't his arm disproportionate?" He pointed toward my figure's elbow, which I'd rendered at an almost uncomfortable angle.

"Maybe that's intentional."

"And what would be the purpose behind that?"

"I'm trying to make the viewer feel cramped."

"You're alienating your audience."

"I don't have an audience."

"Well, how do you know? Who is this for?"

"I don't know, Dad. Maybe it's just for me. Is that all right with you? Maybe I don't want other people to look at it. Or maybe it's not fucking finished yet."

"Language!" he scolded me. *Language*. Had there ever been a more obvious term uttered? "Do you hear that?" he yelled to my mother. "Do you hear what's coming out of your daughter's mouth?" As I left the room, I made a show of crumbling the sketch he'd been lambasting before tossing it to his feet, a last-ditch attempt at provocation. "I think in pictures!" he called after me. "I would say that grants me the credibility to know how an arm should look!"

This exchange was tame compared to the fights we had after he admitted to having had an affair. He didn't tell my mother until after they were separated. Apparently, it had been a dalliance from years prior, so Mom dismissed its weight, allowing it to absorb into the density of her other disappointments. I, however, felt the event was recent enough to punish my father anew. The summer preceding my freshman year of college, I didn't speak a single word to him, which he read as my inability to hear, rather than my refusal to listen. Unwilling to let his rage diminish, he filtered it through another outlet: my decision to study at an academic university in New York rather than an art school in California.

"We need to discuss this," he would say, as if such an adamant tone would perform the incantation necessary to render me willing to consider his appeals. I would blink at him, overly patient, righteously judgmental, silent as a tower. "Why don't you *say* something?" he'd snap at me. "Too afraid I'll talk you out of it? No courage behind those rash convictions?" He was baiting me but I refused to bite. In light of his confession, I wanted to rub his face in every conversation we'd ever had about choice. I wanted to scream that he'd always had it both ways, that he'd been shortchanging everyone involved, except himself. But I wasn't the shouting type. So I swallowed it. I kept quiet and I kept angry. His infidelity was palpable. It was something I could clutch to my chest and point to whenever I doubted the rationale of a grudge long-held.

Such doubts arose from my memories of early childhood, back when my father and I had been best friends. As a kid, I perceived nothing but his selfless devotion to his work and his family. He'd kept everything in order and still made time for me, which I'd eagerly accepted. But, as I got older, I saw that fall away. I saw that his work monopolized his time and that he allowed it to be so. In addition to writing, filming, and editing, his meetings, parties, and premieres took precedence over our birthdays, anniversaries, and holidays. The hardest part was his constant presence despite his absence. We watched him on TV all the time: interviews, documentaries, promotional shorts. We saw the person that the public adored, but the flash bulbs left us dazed and, during his sporadic visits home, he seemed indistinct at best.

In an attempt to make his itinerancy seem normal, Mom acted like it was nothing. For years, I followed suit. Why should I complain when she seemed fine? But with age, she lost her finery, as it were. Her spirit fell into disrepair and, as she grew to expect less and less from him, I grew to loathe his every move, silent at first, until I reached the age of adolescent criticism and lost the ability to hold my tongue. I began to pick apart everything he did; how he dressed, what he ate, with whom he spent his time. As I became more vocal about his flaws, he served it back at me. The difference was that I was a teenager, so my defensive tactic was to mumble, which he often answered with, "Speak up, would you? I can't understand you unless you're willing to enunciate." Couple that with my raging hormones and my tendency to cry when embarrassed and you had the second act of a Russian tragedy. Naturally, he viewed my sobbing through the lens of a director. Impatient and unmoved, he often asked, "Are you through?" The implication that I could shut off my feelings invariably made me cry harder and regardless of the number of times we had the same argument, the matter was never resolved. He would get frustrated and shut down and I would vacillate between haughty pig-headedness and a deep-seated fear of being wrong.

His legacy had brainwashed me. I was scared of his success, scared of becoming someone different, someone detestable. I didn't want anything so grand as notoriety; I only wanted more time to figure out how (and who) to be. The divine grail that everyone wants at every stage of life: more time. So I stood on the teetering precipice between childhood yearning and adult responsibility and promised myself to make him believe that I could do what I pleased without definitively deciding anything. Failing that, I would establish a foundation for myself as a "professional," thus proving him wrong about my "art." Armed with those jumbled, contrary ideals, I began college.

My plan was to major in English, with a minor in studio art as my compromise. "That's a very considerate gesture," my mother said of my almost-decision. But my lack of resolve had little to do with consideration. I needed options; my father needed to be right. We both came up a few breaths short of mollification.

To be fair, I regarded English the same way my father regarded my performance in school. I assumed it would be a successful venture with no cajoling or coaxing required. My gift for the written language was therefore mine to exploit, so English wound up playing my plain, reliable pal while I recklessly wooed its smarter, prettier counterpart: linguistics. How I reveled in the existence of the International Phonetic Alphabet, how well its symbols fit my mouth. I used to read them aloud, believing that if I could pronounce them all, I could make any word in any language come true—or at least *sound* true. Drunk with the power of speech, I fell steadfastly in love with a field I knew nearly nothing about. I would be a phonetician. It seemed the surest thing in the world.

After officially declaring my major, I very deliberately decided not to tell my father. "There," I thought. "That's two decisions made." My mother begrudgingly promised not to give me away, but convinced me to break it to him gently when next we met. I agreed, though our next meeting haplessly occurred after the divorce had been filed but before it had been finalized.

The divorce disrupted my life in ways I couldn't comprehend. It had snuck in through a window ajar and, though my 'valuables' had been left unsupervised, it bypassed them altogether, deciding instead to steal all the food. As a result, I relied on a type of self-cannibalism for base survival.

When my father appeared in New York, visiting for business purposes, he insisted that we meet. I declined, citing our mutually busy schedules, but he reasoned that he would be working near my apartment and classes. Also, he was not above paying exorbitant cab fare if I was on the other side of town. Somehow, in a city of nearly eight million people, I had no chance of avoiding him.

I considered making up a prior engagement out of spite—after all, it had been my mother alone who had informed me of the divorce—but his meetings went on for days. He would have eventually seen through my lie. So we met for lunch where he was just as garrulous as ever. The topics of discussion included the movie, the weather, his flight, the difference between the east and west coasts, and whether life really was as bubbly and grandly insipid as it appeared.

I nibbled and stewed and lost my appetite.

"Why don't we have that wrapped up for you, hmm?" He was already waving his hand for the server. I wanted him to stop. I wanted him to let me in. I wanted him to admit his shortcomings and realize his errors. But we revealed nothing. I stood and walked to the restroom. Had I been able to drown myself in the toilet, I would have done it just to get his name in the tabloids.

On our way back to my dorm, in the cab he insisted we take, there was much knee patting and urging on his part for me to tell him about school. And for each word I offered, he repaid it with five. A bargain hunter's dream.

Finally, when we were safely in the confines of my room, I uttered my longest sentence of the afternoon. "I dropped my art minor." He released an impatient little breath, half a *tsk*, half a sigh. "I just thought you should know."

With a shake of his head, my father laid his hand on my forearm. "You'll go back to it." I felt like a cancer victim being told my hair would eventually regrow. Shortly thereafter, we exchanged our stiff parting pleasantries and I showed him the door.

After he left, I ransacked the room, hunting for my drawings. Two canvases, four notebooks, and dozens of looseleaf studies could be found thrust into textbooks, shoved into drawers, tucked under my bed, or folded into the pockets of coats and the palms of unworn gloves. I cringed at the sight of them—at the state of them. Every slight and snide remark he'd ever dealt about my work was true. But this realization only fueled my desire to be rid of them.

Reminders invariably lead to nostalgia, which leads to time wasted. Looking ahead while also looking back, I crafted a plan to destroy them in an uncharacteristic bout of grandeur. I gathered all my pieces, everything I could find, and built a pyre on the shore of Port Washington to send them astray—*astray* is only one letter from *ashtray*. As the embers caught each flickering corner, I choked back my regret. I had to rebuild myself. I had to start clean.

Unfortunately, this token gesture was hardly revolutionary. I needed something bigger, something permanent. Trusting only one person in matters regarding my father, I buckled down and called my mother.

"You destroyed all your work?"

"Mom." There was too much. It was too soon. "That's—not the point."

"Well, what is the point?"

"I need you to help me think. I don't know what to do now. I want to start over, but I don't know how to properly begin."

"Dear, there's not going to be anything proper about it."

I clenched my jaw, frustrated and flummoxed.

"Mom, can you just say what you mean? I don't speak Parable."

Her tone grew humored at my flippancy. "What I mean

is that there isn't a right or wrong way to do this. Just go and live. Take some time to figure out what makes you happy."

"*Nothing* makes me happy."

"Well, you can't have *nothing*." My mother, ever the wordsmith.

"You know what I mean."

"I do. But give it some thought, despite the semantic aerobics. You already have everything. If you really want less, figure out what that means, exactly. Figure out what you want to subtract."

To have less. What to subtract. I longed for a place where my father couldn't reach me or, barring that, one where he mattered significantly less, one where I wouldn't be so often reminded of his ever-present influence on my life. Did that mean a complete purge of everything that reminded me of him or did it mean taking time away from the man himself? I was too scattered to say for sure. I had to nail down my certainties.

Who was I without my father?

My father named me. My mother wanted my name to be Agatha, a choice that would have rooted me in a different era, holding lofty, yet geriatric ideals for myself. But my father railed against it. The person I am now is grateful to him. Agatha has no chance of diminution. Taking it syllabically,

A sounds like a subtle shock, a tiny apathetic yelp; *Gath* bears too close a resemblance to a truncated version of *catheter* as uttered by a deaf Russian; and *a*, (pronounced *uh*, most common of all dialogue markers), gets a wretched reputation from chronic stutterers and is almost as ubiquitous as *like* among the under-40 crowd.

None of these fit me at all, neither in part nor sum. Instead, my father chose Meredith, from which I culled *Mere*.

> mere – *adj.* – Having no greater extent, range, value, power, or importance than the designation implies; that is barely or only what it is said to be

Only what it is said to be. I chose this adjective eons ago, as mine to shoulder when nothing else suited me. How fitting that I wrought such a name from my father.

Oddly enough, I did know an Agatha, off and on, for several years. We met during my time at NYU and we parted the way clouds so often will: not so much with distance, but with silence over time.

Agatha was an actor, just like everyone else in New York. But unlike everyone else, her choice to act wasn't a desire that arose from vanity. She didn't wither without attention or decide on acting because she had no other marketable skills.

Agatha was schooled as a mechanical engineer and could have been one by trade, had she pursued it. This distinction set her apart from the teeming mass of would-be actors, singers, dancers, and models who flanked the city's streets on every side. They stole the last seat on the subway. They offered dismissive, bored glances when they encountered each other on the street or in bars or at other social gatherings which didn't require civility. Agatha abhorred these practices, but her scientific training allowed her to view them with the detached interest of a technician determining the latent heat of ice. Her cool surfaced where others' disdain showed through. This won her a few devoted followers, as well as some fine enemies, but she was phlegmatic and confident enough that she recognized the situation for the windfall it was and she used to leave for auditions as if marching into war. If she emerged the victor, it was one more credit on her resume; if not, she regrouped to double her efforts. All the same, a coup for her often resulted in the loss of a friend who vied for the same role. This riled her.

"I don't begrudge them their parts," she would say. Agatha was emphatically logical about the process. The facet that inspired her to stand with dignity on the D train or smile at the others' contempt in Village dives was the same attribute that let her figure the odds of landing any part. She always factored the weight of the competition and it was always her drive that pushed her to stay the course.

Such estimable courage drew me to her, since it was a quality I sorely lacked. New York would've eaten me alive had it not been for her. Functioning as my example of successful transplantation—Agatha was born and bred in Iowa—I thought she would live in New York indefinitely. I saw her as impervious and even endeared to its abuse, but it wasn't long after our respective twenty-first birthdays when I was disillusioned by her decision to move to Los Angeles.

"Please tell me you're kidding" I said when she told me.

"No joke," she shook her head. "I'm tired of New York. I'm tired of being broke—less than broke. I'm tired of being unable to afford happiness in this miserly burg."

"L.A. isn't going to change that."

"At least there are things to do," was her attempt at reason.

"We're in New York! There's plenty to do!"

"Sure," she laughed humorlessly. "I can continue going to auditions just to hear the sound of my own voice followed by an exhausted, Thanks, but no thanks. I can go on receiving free dinners and MetroCards as payment for background work in shitty student films. I could become the first acting busker in Central Park. I could become a mime."

I had no answer for that.

"You can't go to L.A.," I groaned. "It'll ruin you forever."

"Then it'll finish the job New York already started." She was beaten down. I could understand that. It's why I'd left

California in the first place.

"You don't understand," I told her, "you think New York is bad, but L.A. is absurdist. Time doesn't even make sense there."

"Mere, what are you talking about?"

"No one ages! The years go by and people just get younger!"

"That's not true."

"It *is.* And it's always summer. There are no seasons. It's sunny all the time and the sun sets on the wrong side of the land."

"The sun sets over the water."

"My point exactly!" I was shouting now, overcome at the thought of losing her."Even the sky is in on it! It's this awful pinkish-blue color, just like cotton candy—"

"I love cotton candy," she declared.

"You would. It's so cloying."

"You don't mean that," she said, her voice calm. She refused to argue with me.

"I do mean it," I pouted. She sidled up next to me and laid her head against my neck.

"Be happy for me?" I could feel her voice searching for forgiveness; it was the closest thing I'd get to an apology.

"I can't," I said. "You're the only sane person I know and you're throwing it all away."

I heard her blink and sensed her grin; it was the closest

thing she'd get to absolution.

Agatha was one of the main reasons for my return to California. However, the ultimate reason I stayed was because of Patrick. Somehow or other, life kept throwing us together.

"Well, well, well, if it isn't *ma petite Merde...*"

"Up your ass, Patrick."

"Where I'd prefer you, always."

After leaving home, I only ever swore around Patrick. It was my shortcoming; he made me feel foolish when I wanted him to find me astute, adept, stunning, and otherwise brilliant. Not brilliant in that everyday, British usage of the term; rather, I wanted him to consider me exceptional. I wanted to hear him say, "I think you're smart."

I blamed my need for Patrick's adoration on our undergraduate rivalry. That and our occasional, unbalanced, raucous affair. It became a vendetta. Our disagreements occurred often enough to be not just memorable, but legendary, in both volume and scope. We waged verbal combat with ease, caring neither for our hewn down egos nor dismantled bonds. Other people can afford to be thoughtless; they're ignorant of the gravity their speech holds. But linguists will devastate if only because we can do so with a well-placed term or phrase. Then it's the silences that serve as our minions. They scrape at wounds old and new, where apologies dare not tread.

It's exponentially worse with phoneticians, which both Patrick and I longed to be at the time. I could always tell when he'd stopped listening to what I was saying, not because of disinterest, but because he was dissecting my pronunciation. While this drove me mad, I couldn't say I'd never done it. When presented with an interesting dialect, the subject matter is entirely irrelevant (though the speaker rarely agrees). Such disagreements often lead to raised voices or to swearing, which takes me back to Patrick. My filthy little weaknesses: Patrick and profanity. They clasp hands and skip back and forth, the latter out of my mouth, the former into it. I was a feeble wretch around him because he caused me to lose all manner of speech.

He made me forget my words.

My first fight with Patrick held some eerily familiar—familial?—undertones. We'd been working on an arbitrarily enforced group project involving the evolution of socioeconomic varieties (*dialects* or *accents*) among targeted ethnic groups; in other words, accents influenced by money, accents influenced by race (which are influenced by money), and accents influenced by class (which are influenced by money). Given that the original files to which we compared our findings were recorded by our professor when *he* was an undergraduate and that our class was comprised of overbearing, anxious would-be linguists who shouldn't have been emotionally exposed to anyone, much less live human research subjects, our professor's status as a tenured educator seem as ephemeral as steam released from an arctic geyser. This could have been the reason he suggested we work in groups. Pairing one possibly unbalanced student with a potentially sensible one decreased the likelihood of the emotional damage control he would later have to perform.

Or perhaps he was hoping we would systematically destroy one another.

With the samples collected, we were in the midst of the most arduous and time-consuming step of all linguistic research: transcription. To do it quickly meant to risk error and it had to be done correctly in order to hold any weight at all. That said, we shouldn't have cared as much as we did. Neither Patrick nor I knew how to effectively work with another person and our separate desire to do things the "right" way led to a slew of disagreements. I just wanted to do my work and Patrick just wanted it all to be over. According to him, every mistake made was mine—whether it actually was or not didn't matter. In certain ways, I feel like he was trying to pick a fight with me. He derided my materials (an ancient laptop), my methods of order (notes cribbed longhand, with scads of illegible corrections in the margins), and my work ethic (slow, but deliberate). I responded not at all, save a sullen silence. This exasperated him.

"Why do you *do* that?" I didn't answer, which goaded him further. "You just sit there and take it? Put up a fight. Stand your fucking ground. I'd have more respect for you if you'd just—"

"—I'm inured to it," I interrupted him. I was in no mood to be forthcoming about my emotional issues, so I let the conversation lull. If only he'd been content enough to follow suit.

"Well, someone took her Pedant Pills this morning." He was mocking my word choice.

"Blame the GREs," I told him.

"GR*E*," he corrected. "No matter the number of iterations, there's only one exam."

"Listen," I snapped, losing my patience, "what the hell did I ever do to you? Why don't you just leave me alone?" How literal we allow ourselves to be. He tried to leave then, may have even wanted to. He got as far as the hallway, hat in hand, as it were. But I had hurried after him, rushed and panicking. "Don't," the word flew from me, barely syllabic.

He slowed his exit to a standstill and served me a pitiless look. "One of us will have to apologize," he said, apathetic.

"Neither of us would mean it," I replied.

"Apology accepted."

"But I didn't—" I could barely comprehend the easy escape he'd offered before he was pinning me to the wall, hand against my hip, telling me to shut up and making it all meaningless.

After that first time together, Patrick and I didn't talk much. We saw each other in class, but avoided each other afterward, which, confusing silence with mystery, I took as a good sign. My mother wasn't the sort who espoused prudishness in the name of a relationship maintained, but she did tell me early on that a long-lasting romance could easily be achieved by keeping the pursuit interesting.

"You never want to leave them asking for less."

At the time, I wondered at her use of the third person plural. How many of them would there be? By the time I'd met Patrick, I'd had less than a handful of interested parties, nothing serious, but enough to know who *they* were. Enough to feel accomplished over his specific attention. Accomplished, yet unprepared.

Each of our trysts occurred unplanned and ended wordlessly. We never discussed any future meeting, never took our encounters or the situation seriously enough to deem it worthy of conversation. However, I secretly assumed they would keep happening. I could have mutely continued ad infinitum.

Patrick disagreed.

I caught him studying me one evening after I'd gotten redressed. I returned his stare sporadically, my gaze flitting about, landing on furniture and empty air and nothingness, but always rising again to meet his eye.

Many times, I inhaled to speak. I exhaled just as often without sound.

"What?" he asked pointedly.

"I—nothing."

"It's not nothing," he said. "It's very something."

"Yes," I admitted. "I don't want to talk about it."

"Why?" his tone was playful. Now I interested him. Now he was curious.

"I can't. I don't—have the words."

He sniffed and scoffed. "Don't have the words? Which ones do you need, exactly?"

I shrugged one shoulder toward my chin. "The right ones."

"Aren't they all *right*?"

"As often as they're all wrong."

"You're being purposely obtuse."

I shook my head. "I'm not. Words matter. They're remembered and cherished and sometimes used against you."

"In a court of law?"

"Not like that. If you misuse them—if *I* misused them, I could be held accountable. I want to mean what I say or not say anything at all."

"You mustn't talk very often."

"Only when I have something to say." He nodded, already dismissing the notion. "You really don't know how important your words are?" I asked. "You don't know how they affect people?"

"It's all perspective. I don't think they matter. You do. We happen to disagree."

"Don't be cavalier with me. I don't appreciate it."

"I can't help but be cavalier," he argued. "You care more about this than I do. Were you to become upset over it, I would simply pat your shoulder and say, 'There, there,' until you got over it."

"But I wouldn't."

"Yes, you would."

"I wouldn't." My expression was as insistent as my tone. "You just—you don't understand. I can't *not* care."

"You're so sure of that? Have you ever tried?"

What I thought, but didn't say was, "My entire life."

II. Paralysis

These memories irk me. They're akin to reading *loose* where the word should be *lose*. I can feel my veins tighten, sense my heart work that much harder to accommodate the heightened pressure. I acknowledge that I'm always inches away from this state and it quickly ebbs. Even after I settle down, I'm resentful that my father still affects me this way.

Afraid that I'll abandon the trip altogether, I force myself to think of other things on the remainder of the drive. It isn't until I'm outside of my father's house that I freeze. I feel like a call girl with a noticeable sore on her mouth. I dial Eliot.

"I don't think I can do this."

"Nonsense," comes his assured voice, "I'll come pick you up. It'll be fine."

"No. I'm already here."

"Well, what's wrong?" If Eliot feels any impatience, he keeps it out of his tone.

"I can't get out of my car. I think I have vertigo."

"Mer—" he says, pronouncing it as *mare.*

"—Mere."

"*Meredith.* You're going to be fine. I'll come out to meet you." His voice becomes quieter, farther away. "I have to go meet someone outside. Relax, I'll be right back." He was talking to my father. They were discussing me as if I couldn't hear. It put me in mind of my parents. They had very different opinions regarding child rearing. It's a shame there's not a compatibility test for such things.

Eliot leans over the driver's side of my windshield, cupping his hands around his eyes and peering within.

"All the better to see you with," he stumbles blindly for some levity.

"I think I might throw up if I go in there," I tell him.

"Like the normal kind of vomiting? Or the Linda Blair projectile kind of vomiting?" I nod absently at his clarification. "Have you ever seen that movie?" Eliot, such a slave to his profession. Then again, so am I.

"I think it would be the normal kind," I say, ignoring his other question. "That's bad enough."

"Why don't you come inside?" Eliot's voice changes. I can hear the syrup oozing. I know that tone is usually kept under wraps, save for the particularly hard clients who need to be wooed, whose contracts are integral. For the seven-figure deals, or for the hard-won six-figure ones. He'd used it to coax my father.

I abhor this sort of persuasion. I feel it's beneath him. I sigh loudly and out tumbles my irritability.

"What do you have staked in this?" I grouse. "Why does it matter?"

A pause. He doesn't want to tell me. He glances once, twice toward the house before setting his gaze to the floor.

"Gary passed away last year."

His son. Younger than me...than I am...was. Am.

My cold fingertips meet my burning mouth. "I'm sorry." I shouldn't have pressed him. I consider backpedaling. I consider attempting to comfort him. I consider peeling out of there and ramming my car, face first, into the nearest sturdy tree. Instead, I dumbly apologize. Again. It gets me out of the car.

I wonder if my father will greet me cordially or if he'll civilly dismiss me. I'm not sure which I'd prefer. If it were when last I knew him, I would definitely bet on the former. I can only remember one time when he'd ever been rendered speechless.

*

We hadn't spoken in weeks. Not over the phone, nor

through any passive-aggressive messages relayed through my mother, who always gallantly delivered them without complaint. It wasn't long after the divorce had been finalized and they were divvying up the particulars. Who would live where? What amount of money would change hands and when?

I had gone home for my mother. I didn't give a damn what my father would keep. He wasn't the one in need.

He had arrived home after an absence of only a few days—I imagined him staying in a hotel, oh the glamorous shame of it all—but he'd likely been away for business. I confronted him as soon as our eyes met.

"Why did you do it?"

This stood for several things: Why did he desert us? Why hadn't he tried harder? Why wasn't he with Mom when she told me about the divorce? It was their joint responsibility, just as I had always been. I admit that my response was delayed. I cede that my thoughts should have been voiced months prior, years prior, sometime—anytime—before that moment. But I'm not quick-witted. I need time to ruminate. Most people accept this and give me time to think before I speak. So rarely do I allow them the same courtesy.

"Answer me," I wanted his brash eloquence, would have welcomed it as part and parcel of his explanation.

My father chose a point just below my sternum, but far past it, perhaps within it, to set his eyes upon. Before his gaze returned to mine, his left eyebrow lifted, the most infinitesimal of shrugs, his exhale acting as punctuation.

"There's nothing to say."

He left me then, by backing away and exiting whence he came.

My final year of school, I helped Agatha pack her books and memories away. Before her departure, she asked me to tell her about California.

"Why? You've already been there." My response was purposely dour.

"But you're *from* there," she said. "I want to hear about it from *you*."

"You want to hear about L.A. or about the entire thing?"

"I want to hear about all of it—the whole Sunshine State."

"That's Florida. California's the Golden State."

"Just tell me."

"California is—expansive. And expensive. And weary and hot. It's got a reputation for luring gobs of people in with promises of gold and fame, but accepting only a select few."

"Say it isn't so!" she cringed.

I continued, "Those in L.A. are particularly susceptible to the tough love bait-and-switch. Movie premieres are exciting things until you realize you're only there to accentuate the carpet."

"Everybody's part of the crowd," she said.

"Just don't end up part of the scenery."

"Don't worry. The Guild pays for background work."

"You'd get typecast as the silent girl. Trust me when I say it's a thankless job," I warned her.

She smiled at me with sympathy, "Happens to the best of them."

"Speaking of being cast off," I went on, "the very ground might reject you at any moment—earthquakes go against all etymological logic: terra *firma*—and the sun emits dangerous, invisible rays that will likely render your skin ragged."

"There's always plastic surgery," Agatha posited.

"You'll fit right in."

"What else?" she goaded me.

"What else," I repeated. "California is not for introverts. It tugs at you, yanking down any guard or protection you might have had and leaves you exposed. It plays tug-of-war with inhibitions, pushing you into the outside, to coin an oxymoron."

"Nicely done," she said.

"Thanks. Regarding phonetics, the vowel sounds of native Californians are particularly interesting—"

"Let's skip over this part," Agatha urged. She was often the sounding board for my phonetic leanings.

I digressed, "In California, it never snows on Christmas and, despite what television would have you believe, very few people can afford to have snow flown in."

"I'll decorate the palm trees with snow from a can."

"Just when I thought California couldn't get classier." Here, she laughed. "And last, but certainly not least, I wish I weren't from there. Rather, I wish I were from some sane place where people acted normally. I retract that, actually. Some sane place where people don't act at all—no offense. Where people behave honestly and bravely when they've screwed up."

"I'm not sure such a place exists," Agatha said.

"Neither am I."

Graduation arrived on a cloud free of rain. I proceeded down the aisle in cap and gown, then recessed with my blank, bound scroll in hand. The same way words stand for ideas, this unmarked page was a symbol, a placeholder for their gratitude; much like the ceremony itself, the paper was only a gesture.

Congratulations, you've done something. Thank you for paying to learn.

I clutched their unwritten gesture, gripped it next to my heart. Its edges fluttered when pinned to my pulse, beating a rapid cadence, so charged was the setting and each glance and the often uttered notion, "What next?" Everyone had asked in one way or other. Somehow, graduation hadn't been enough. It lacked finality. We remained unfinished, unending. Something was sure to follow; if only it would reveal itself.

"How does it feel?" A new question to rouse me from my depths. Standing at my side, with jacket and loosened tie under his open gown, was Patrick. "Hello."

"Hi," I said. "I didn't see you during the procession." Not for lack of trying. I was a rubbernecker, but too short to see past the crowd.

"Too many damned people," he said.

"So," I sought a prompt, anything that would hold his attention. "Is yours blank too?" I looked toward his neatly rolled page, cinched with a sealed ribbon.

"I'm afraid so." He unraveled it to show me. "I paid eighty thousand dollars and all I got was this lousy education."

"Ha."

"Your family here?" he asked.

"My Mom, yeah. Yours?"

"My parents are around. Would you like to meet them?"

I grimaced, "Do you think we're ready for that?"

"No."

"Do you know where they are?"

"I could call and find out," he said, stolid.

"Is it honestly worth the trouble?"

"Probably not. And it would force us into an awkward goodbye."

So it was goodbye. "In that case, I would very much like to avoid meeting your parents." We shared our first genuine smile, but the occasion made it brief. "What'll we do now?" I asked.

"Question of the hour."

"I know." Patrick inhaled deeply and exhaled a shrug. "Is your room packed yet?"

"No."

"Could we?"

His sheets felt like homecoming, his skin as fine as breath. Once we were separate, he asked, "Will you stay in New York for grad school?"

"I'm not sure I'll go to grad school," I told him.

"Don't be stupid. What else would you do?"

This sobered me, helped me find my clothes. "Wait," he said. "Don't take it that way. You know what I meant."

"Yes. I know exactly what you meant." I was not yet livid but I had to fight to choose the least loaded words. "My decisions are not stupid."

"I would hardly call avoiding graduate school a decision."

"I'm not avoiding it. I just want to explore my other options."

"Like living off of Mommy and Daddy?"

He couldn't have hurt me more had he struck me. In two

sentences, the gloves were off.

"I could live off of them here, if I chose to do so. But there's not a single reason I have to stay in New York."

Agatha found work almost immediately upon arriving in Los Angeles. She landed a soap opera role and commercial voice-overs and all sorts of television work. I've never had the attention span for TV. I need something long-form to hold my interest. Or at least something that gives me a reason to come back, a quality I often find lacking in sitcoms and medical dramas.

My father shared similar aversions to television, though that often had to do with writing. "Writing for television is useless," he would say. "You're beholden to censors, sponsors, and worst of all, an implacable audience." I sometimes hated that his thoughts and opinions aligned with my own, though my linguistics training helped me to understand and cope with that.

When acquiring our first languages, each of us is allotted a number of years to build our varieties, or accents. Everything contributes to it: parents, teachers, friends, the media, your neighbors—all of it combines to create every odd pronunciation and idiosyncratic term, which encompasses your unique linguistic profile.

Around your fifteenth birthday, and some linguists say

even sooner, the ability to change your variety becomes nearly impossible. Anyone who has ever attempted to learn a foreign language in adulthood can attest to yearning for "perfect" speech. We want to sound like native speakers and we want it to come naturally, however affected our speech patterns might actually be.

On a similar note, if you subscribe to the school of thought that says your environment directly contributes to your personality (just like your variety), the same can be said for your learned quirks (just like a learned accent). Starting with childhood, you have a set of stimuli that casts a mold for you to contort within. So, if you're an only child and you have a doting parent, odds are you may wind up with an overinflated sense of entitlement. Or, if you're the eldest of many children and are forced to step into a parental role at a young age, you'll probably become a nurturer as an adult. It's all case-sensitive and there are no hard and fast rules that apply to everyone, but it's with these thoughts in mind that I can deduce the logic behind my own eccentricities.

The short version is that I get all my wordy quirks from my schooling and, prior to that, from my mother. My father's eloquence didn't quite reach me and nearly all similarities that we do share, I avoid discussing, not because I don't acknowledge their existence—I fully admit that they're there—but because I've tried so acutely to alter them. What bothers me most is that, even now, after having spent the same number of years away from him as the number of years he spent rearing me and shaping my personality, I still feel my father's fingerprint on my actions. I can still sense his presence in my gaze and step and demeanor.

He and I will always speak the same language, lending my own variety practically no variation at all. I'm lucky enough to have my very own impediment though. I brought it all the way back from the other side of the world.

After talking to my mother and weighing my post-baccalaureate options, I found that what I wanted—solidarity, for lack of a more concise term—could not be had in the U.S. My most lucrative option was teaching English in China.

"I could do that," I told myself. *Could* became *would* became *will*, and shortly after the interview process, I found myself eager to tell someone about my bold new future. My Mom already knew, as did Agatha, and I didn't want to tell my father because I knew the exchange would be in some way disappointing.

I opened my phone with intent to call Patrick, then stopped. I was still angry, still hurt, still not ready for a mutual conversation. An e-mail would have been too impersonal, a letter too formal. In the end, I sent a postcard from New York to New York. *Going to China*, I wrote. *Hope your applications are going well. Mere*

With no logical reason to stay, I left the country, adamant

that I was making the right decision.

For three months, I made a concerted effort to be self-sufficient. I was gainfully employed and supporting myself. I was making consistent payments toward my student loans. Also, I had no one to talk to and plenty of time to think, both of which led to my near death of homesickness. To make matters worse, my body never adjusted to the time difference, so I functioned on a few hours of sleep each afternoon. At some point, I'd taken to alcohol-induced slumber. Just as I was drifting off, my cheeks would start to tingle, as if they'd fallen asleep or been overworked from laughter. Six days before I left China, it felt more like burning than tingling, but I was too tired to care.

When I woke later that evening, the right side of my face was dry and flaky. Reaching for my cheek, I realized that the flaking on my skin had once been saliva. After a brief bout of shame, I stumbled to the bathroom to wash my face. The room I rented did not have a private bathroom, so I was reduced to sharing my humiliation in the community restroom, replete with sickly florescent lighting that rendered even the ruddiest complexion peaked.

Somehow, I didn't notice my face's unfamiliar state until I threw water into my unclosed right eye. I laughed a bit, thinking I was still a little drunk. I tried to wet my face again, and still, my right eye did not shut. Looking up to examine it, the full view of my face appeared in the mirror. The right side sagged, as if it had aged four decades in as many hours. With the tip of my middle finger, I pushed my right eyelid shut. I removed my finger and my eye opened.

My blinks became winks.

My chest heaved.

I vomited into the sink and blacked out.

When I woke, I remember feeling feverish one moment, then ice cold the next. I lay on the floor and feared the mirror. More specifically, I feared the me who occupied it. I told myself all the stereotypical things:

This isn't happening.

It's not real.

It's a trick. An optical illusion or perhaps a drunken dream.

"A trick," I said aloud.

My voice was a foreigner: an ugly term, but well-suited to the situation. I grunted and tugged myself up to face my reflection. My voice was in there somewhere. My real voice. I stared at myself, winking. I said my name, most familiar of all spoken sounds, and watched my mouth strain as I uttered it.

"Meredith. Mer-e-dith. *Mere.*"

I recited as much as I could remember of Longfellow's poem, *The Midnight Ride of Paul Revere.* I'd had to memorize it in grade school and could still recall long jags. But it all sounded wrong. All my words—the ones I adored enough to call mine—fell from my mouth, mangled and off-kilter. If asked at that moment, I couldn't properly explain the situation, not for any lack of understanding or willingness on my part, but because I could barely stand the sounds I emitted. I imagine that the disdain I felt was similar to a xenophobe's feelings about the non-native's tongue. Yet my voice's pronunciation belonged to no ethnic group. Rather, it was beholden to the makeshift, bastardized whims of my stiff jaw and dead lip.

I envisioned myself at work, holding a hypothetical position now forever removed from my grasp. I imagined my limp mouth bracing around a full vowel: a round O. I could hear the sound properly, could form it within my mouth, behind my teeth, supported by my tongue. But it came forth flat, bearing something akin to stigma. My palate was worse than cleft; it was irreparably sullied.

Turning away from the mirror, I took up my lips between my right thumb, index and middle finger, and I twisted. Held fast, I thought I could shock my mouth into restoring itself to its former state, just as I could force a child, who played dead, into living by holding his nostrils closed.

I clamped my lips together until my thumb ached. When I finally released them, a purplish-red sore appeared as a mirrored lip-print across my mouth. A kiss of death. The kiss-off. So many idioms, none of them enough. Like the backward child I was and am, I felt there was only one just punishment for my mouth: ignorance. I pretended it didn't exist. I stopped feeding it. I would starve it out. I stamped back to my room and, holding my hand over my right eye, tried to go to sleep.

Hours passed. Maybe half a day. When my stomach shuddered, I fed it dank water. I purposely ate from unwashed dishes. Had I been able to get them down, I would have eaten rocks. This treatment didn't last long. I woke from a fitful sleep, utterly nauseated and ready to confess any and every sin I'd ever committed. Less than a day later, I was in a Chinese emergency room, which is much like an American waiting room with complimentary IV bags. I felt like a headless dress form who'd been stuck with a microphone stand as her prom date. I kept glancing from it to the other patients who'd been corralled around me.

In the absence of my own wretched voice, I was made aware that the normal hum of hospital spaces was absent here. It had been replaced by a buzzing chorus of IV stands on wheels, crowds of murmured questions in a language for which I held only a meager understanding, and under that, the perpetual drone of a thousand breathing lungs. It was deafening. Before long, I was talking myself blue in the face. Waffling between whispered pleas and stern reprimands, between "This is what you get. What did you expect, you idiot?" and "I'm sorry... I'm so *sorry.*" I must have seemed schizophrenic.

Finally, I fell silent. I rocked back and forth manically, gripping my IV stand for support. My lungs struggled to expand and contract, to swell and collapse. I tried to ignore the beating of my heart—the steady cadence of my breath—because, once I'd started, I was convinced that if I stopped paying attention to it, those organs would stop functioning. In an effort to distract myself, and to keep my mind from skipping off a cliff, I sang. Softly and poorly, I sang a squeaky rendition of "Stand by Me," dedicated to my own fragility.

No, I won't be afraid.
No, I won't be afraid.
Just as long as you stand, stand by me...

The part about not shedding tears seemed too much like a lie, so I repeated those words until they lost all meaning.

Slowly—slow enough that I couldn't resist it—my mind drifted. I'll call it a hallucination, though I've never been so lucid. I saw myself surrounded by bed sheets the color of barren ice. My bed lay flat against the wall, not in a Murphy fashion, but with its legs perpendicular to the wall's surface as if held there by gravity. The blankets, however, held to no such law. They fell away from me, exposing my tender calves, my feet, and my untouched behind.

My mind shook off its sluggish state and I took a firm tone with myself. "This is *not* happening. You are in China. You are in an emergency room. You are on the ground, as you've always physically been."

Except when flying.

I grunted in frustration. I needed something foolproof, something logic couldn't circumvent. I was beginning to feel a draft at my back, oddly enough, far removed from the most commonly known definition of *backdraft*.

"Please," I said to myself and everyone else within earshot, because I felt it safe enough to do so. "If I get through this, I'll go back." I winced and let out staggered air through my clenched jaw. "I'll make amends." Miniature torrents sweated from my eyes. "I'll right everything that was," here I paused, "*left*."

I slipped away then, into unconsciousness, where I was allowed to uncoil.

I woke with regained strength, possibly even better than before I'd left New York. "Thank you," I said to the person at my side—another patient—who looked at me with an ignorant blink.

I felt for my right eye. It was still there and still open.

When I returned to the States, it was January. I landed in New York because I technically still lived there. It was strange being on the east coast during a crisis. I thought of calling my mother, though that would've required too much explanation. I couldn't see her then. I couldn't see anyone.

I opted to stick it out. I had some money left from teaching and some funds I'd been awarded upon graduation. It was winter and I was in a city that breeds anonymity.

Snow can be described as a weather phenomenon. Not for its unpredictability—meteorologists can spot its patterns from hundreds of miles away—but for its complete re-rendering of a cityscape, for its removal of side streets, rivers, railways, and especially buildings. The altered visibility recasts skyscrapers as a slowly stumbling mob, lurching and leaning and on the precipice of collapse.

Snow made me appreciate the view of Manhattan from the platform of Queensboro Plaza. I wished to be among the buildings, being silently erased.

Maybe if I stood in the right—wrong—part of town at the right—still wrong—time, I could be stabbed to death without a witness or a word.

No one would even know I was gone.

Agatha called me ten days after I got back. I had e-mailed her in an effort to combat depression, but couldn't get beyond a few vague lines about being back in New York.

"Mere!" her voice spoke of another era.

"Agatha." I tried to sound excited. Immediately failing that, I tried to sound like my old self. She begged me to visit her, promised she would make California pleasant. At this show of unexpected affection, I couldn't maintain my cool. Practically sobbing into the phone, I asked if I could call her back.

"No, you can't call me back!" she mother-henned me. "Tell me what's wrong."

"I will." Sniffle, snivel, drip, drip. "I promise. I just—need a minute."

I took down her number and went to wash my face. Once I'd calmed down, I called Agatha and told her I'd had an accident. Nothing serious, just something that prevented me from flying.

"Then I'll come to you!" she said. "I miss you."

"You'd come back to New York?"

"Not permanently," she said. "But I could handle a visit, no problem. New York is easier to deal with when you don't have to be in a certain place at a specific time, so it doesn't matter when you get caught behind a plague of tourists and stay-at-home Moms who never actually stay at home, but instead crowd the subways with two lane strollers and a gaggle of kids and giant dogs and other little dogs that they keep in their purses and—"

"—Agatha?" I interrupted.

"Yes?"

"Try to remember that I still live here."

"Oh. Right."

I knew I couldn't talk her out of visiting, so I didn't bother trying. She flew in via La Guardia, then cabbed to my place because she assumed I wasn't well enough to meet her at the airport. I greeted her at the door wearing a coat and scarf, the latter wrapped around the lower half of my face.

"Are we not staying?" she asked upon seeing my bundled layers.

"I'm just cold."

"Do you have a fever? Have you been to a doctor? Well, I mean, of course you have. What happened anyway?"

She waited patiently for my response, her face wide and clear and open and perfectly symmetrical. I couldn't tell her. I couldn't say it aloud.

Carefully, I opened my coat and unraveled my scarf. Folding it twice over, I set the scarf across my thighs. With one unsteady finger pointing to my mouth and then my eye, I explained. "Bell's Palsy—it happened when I was in China." She walked toward me, squinting at discrete sections of my face. I felt so uncomfortable, I had to fill the space with something. "And I gave myself food poisoning."

That stopped her. "You *gave* yourself food poisoning?"

"It made sense at the time."

She extended her hand, fingers splayed, toward my face, asking, "May I?" I nodded, unable to adequately communicate my fear. I'd only been touched by doctors since the paralysis. "Is it permanent?"

"Only time will tell."

She traced a semi-circle next to the corner of my mouth, then placed a thumb between the outer point of my right eyebrow and right eye. Gently, she tugged the skin upward.

"Can you see out of both eyes?"

"Yes."

With no warning, Agatha leaned forward and kissed the corner of my eye. I watched it happen because I literally could not close my eye to it.

"That should help it heal," she said. I could've sworn a nerve twitched under all my numbness. Maybe it would always feel that way, paralysis as one drawn out spasm—how horrifying. From the concern in Agatha's voice, I likely looked appropriately horrific. "Does it hurt?" she asked.

I forced myself to consider her question. What did *hurt* actually mean? First I said, "Yes." Then, "And no. Physically, it's numb. I'd probably forget about it if I could. If it didn't look like someone poured a new face over my old one and let it drip dry, if it weren't impossible to sleep without my arm covering my eyes, if I could somehow forget the way words should sound—then I think it might hurt less." That was the most I'd said since coming home. Just the sound of it, the disparity between the voice in my head and the voice out of it, made me want to give up speech altogether.

Agatha barely noticed. She blinked, her eyes staying shut just long enough to reveal a wince. "How are your parents taking it?"

"They're not," I said.

"You haven't told them."

The sound I made was half-sigh, half-grunt. "I'll tell them eventually. Once I figure out how."

Agatha stayed with me for two weeks and, in that time, wore down my defenses against moving home. Her argument was that my family was there, and I needed them now, whether I liked it or not. While I didn't agree that I needed them, I did miss my mother and I couldn't keep my ailment a secret indefinitely. Rather than properly planning my departure from New York, I stacked my mismatched furniture on the curb, packed two suitcases, and donated my books to a local thrift store before jetting from Newark back to Los Angeles. No time for second thoughts, no opportunity for doubling back.

I'll right everything that was left.

Newark had been a frigid twenty-five degrees, so I was thankful to arrive in L.A. in the early morning, as the coldest southern Californian weather lingers right up until dawn. I couldn't bear the idea of an immediately balmy reception. It was midmorning in my mind, but only a little after six when I arrived at my mother's apartment in Burbank. She'd wound up with a trifling sum in the divorce, enough that she might as well have been widowed, though, in a way, I suppose she was since she'd married one man who became another. Regardless, despite its modest size, my mother's space was always hers, every book and table and chair imbued with her taste and purpose, sturdy and reliable. Like object, like possessor.

Knowing that she's always been an early riser, I called out to her after letting myself in. "Hello?" My voice returned hollow and tinny to my ear. I expected her to be in the kitchen, hard at work on a crossword puzzle. But there wasn't even coffee brewing. "Mom?"

Her footsteps materialized then, muffled from behind her closed bedroom door. She emerged drowsy, her hair tousled as it never had been during my childhood, awoken to unexpected familiarity. I couldn't help thinking that we'd both changed for the worse.

"Meredith." Always the full name, no room for correction. "Are you all right?" she asked, choosing the one question that undoes me whenever I'm struggling to maintain control over my emotions. Paired with our physical and emotional proximity, her concern brought forth a spate of tears.

She shushed me and led me toward a chair. Somewhere between the kitchen and the living room, I abandoned my luggage. Ever the nurturer, my mother fetched a cup of water and some tissues.

"Do you want to talk about it?" I neither spoke nor moved my head. Her measured, staggered breath communicated her concern for me. "Can I do anything?" I compressed my shoulders, then let them fall slack. She held her hand tentatively over the space near my cheek. Gravity allowed us to make contact. I held a tissue over my right eye, keeping it out of sight. "How's New York?"

I knew she was asking out of defeat. Desperate for a conversation or anything that could get me talking, she tried to put me at ease, but it struck me as odd, the concept of talking about a place I no longer occupied.

"I don't know," I answered.

She must have thought I was being difficult.

"Honey, I can't help you if you don't tell me what's wrong." Her gentle tone did not scold.

With a limp hand, I lowered my tissue. I couldn't tell if she knew.

"My mouth," I began, then stopped at her intent stare. She knew.

"Oh dear." She gathered me up in her arms and uttered soothing terms like, "I'm sorry," and, "I'm here."

It was June when I woke one morning to find I had accepted my new face. I no longer checked for improvement, didn't hope for any miraculous reversal; my condition had become rote. Sensing my ease, my mother suggested that I visit my father. I hadn't seen him since returning from the east coast. The idea that he might believe I was still living in New York excited me, made my presence covert.

"I think you should go," Mom told me. "Especially in light of your last visit with him."

"I'd really rather not."

She had broached other topics with me—potential graduate school options, career goals, any path that would lead me out of my self-perpetuating rut—but she had lost, retreated for fear of pushing too hard. I would not be so lucky on this front.

"You need to consider his feelings."

"Why? It's not as if he's ever returned the favor. I think you of all people would understand that." Her features absorbed and reflected the sting of my words. I looked at my lap as if she'd scolded my bad behavior, but her silence was far worse. How fiendish spite allows us to be. This was vitriol meant for him, but my aim was poorly focused. "I'm sorry," I said at last.

"No need," she said, surrendering as if she'd deserved such a slight. Why couldn't I have inherited her humility? Why did I always revert to sticks and stones? "I just thought—"

"It's okay, Mom." I shook my head, unable to bear her

apology over my rashness. "I'll go."

She looked only at my good eye, a measured practice I would watch her perfect, and a relieved smile broke across her face. Ever the peacemaker. Always considering the best of our intentions.

My father's house conspicuously hid among several others within a gated "community" where the common thread was his neighbors' desire to avoid each other as steadfastly as they ignored the gawking passers-by. Rumors blazed about which house belonged to whom, none of which could be verified because their grounds and pools and possibly even their homes went unused. Collectively, they symbolized the basis of what a model neighborhood could have been: in theory, a circle of well-maintained homes. In practice, they were no more than houses.

But what houses they were. Panels and doors that gleamed like incisors, their accents so bright, they ignited at noon, making each sill and knob glimmer with the wealth of the sun. Fastidiously kept lawns filled the spaces between driveways and walkways and paths used as borders that whispered not, "Keep off," so much as, "Keep away." These warnings were not for intruders, but for neighbors next door.

"This is mine. *That* is yours."

It was a case of the grass never being greener.

I approached the intercom to request entry into my father's house. Having not yet purchased a car, I'd arrived on foot, meaning they had either seen me coming from a mile away or mistaken me for a member of the masses who arrived unannounced and unbidden. While I may have been viewed as unwelcome, my father had been expecting me.

"What do you think of the place?" he asked once I'd sat down, offering only my left side to his critical eye. I'd barely glanced around on my way in. My recollection of the neighborhood and his house materialized only after I'd taken the time to replay our exchange during the silent years that followed.

"It's nice," I faltered, "and big." It was large, though not egregiously so. It would have suited a family.

"Yes," he beamed proudly. "Lots of space to work."

"Hmm," I envied workspace, envied work. "How's all that going?" I asked, busying my idle hands and thoughts with a loose string at the hem of my skirt.

"Very well. Going into pre-production on a new project next month. Casting, location booking, all the exciting preliminaries."

"Great."

"And you?" he said, suddenly interested. "What are your plans?"

My response lacked every sort of undertone. "I haven't really got any plans at the moment."

I expected him to lunge at me, to launch a verbal attack decrying my indecisiveness. Perhaps he knew how fully equipped I was to fight back; perhaps he could sense how ready I was to accuse him of having me and my mother and our support and everything else for so many years. It could have been that he knew I considered my indecision hereditary because he sidestepped the entire argument in three words.

"And how's school?" Spoken as if he held no opinion regarding my future at all. It occurred to me then that my mother had likely warned him about my fragile state. This assumption emboldened me, made me care less about his opinions.

"I'm done with school," I said plainly.

"You *quit?*"

"I graduated." He seemed relieved until I mentioned, "A year ago." His features reeled then; he'd missed a milestone. Instantly, he was on his feet, on his toes.

"Congratulations," he said. I stood as well, half expecting him to shake my hand, half wanting to delay his full view of my face.

"Thank you," I said, unsure of where to look to counter his unpredictable panic.

"Are you leaving?" he asked, a reaction to my standing. He inched closer to my right side and I retreated.

"No, I—" Glancing for the exits and finding none nearby,

I hurried verbally forward. "You had stood, so I thought..."

My sinuses lined themselves with fluid; my tear ducts released their reserves. Without any notice, I hastily clawed at my face, apologized, then searched my bag for a tissue. Dabbing at my lids and cheeks, I looked up to find my father had left the room and returned with a pitcher of water.

"Here," he offered a glass to me. "Stop." He meant the rushed cleansing of my face. I took a series of slow breaths, held my hands together to cease their shaking.

I watched as he studied my features, as he assessed the *after* compared to his memorized *before*. Had I full command of my eyes, I would have looked down; instead I turned my face away.

"What?" he said, his concentration broken. "What's wrong?"

"This isn't—" What could I say? This isn't what I came here to do? This isn't how I pictured our next visit to be? Would it have made any difference? I felt like I'd always been on display for him. Like he'd always been analyzing the rawest parts of me. "This isn't *fun* for me, Dad."

"This?" he repeated. "Don't worry about it. This is nothing. This is manageable. We can fix this." *This*. Had he actually acknowledged our relationship as broken? Would we walk the proper path to mend it? "I'll get you the best doctors."

No, not *this*, but "This."

I recoiled from him. "Thank you, but no."

"What?" The very word was incredulity.

"I said *no*." He stared at me, no longer studying my misshapen features, but looking only at my eyes, flummoxed by the anger he saw there.

"Why not?"

"I would think it was obvious, but I've gone through enough."

"You haven't told me anything about what you've gone through," he said. "How am I supposed to know?"

"You didn't even ask me what happened, so I assume Mom told you. Besides, I've never had to tell you anything. You've always formed your own opinions about what I should or shouldn't do."

"I'd say you and I are past that stage."

I released a crooked laugh. "You would." I offered up a sigh, but it emerged as a half-hearted sob. "I should go."

He stepped forward, almost blocking my path. "You just got here!"

"Yes, that's true," was all I could think to say.

"Don't go," he said. "Let me help you. It doesn't matter, what's happened, whatever it was. We could have it fixed." I balked. "No one would have to know."

"*Everyone knows*," I released a yell that had been building for years; I almost couldn't follow it with lesser, gentler sounds. "But even—even if they didn't,

I would know."

Whether that explanation had been enough, he didn't say. I suppose it wouldn't have mattered even if he had. We'd both stopped listening to each other years prior.

In the yellowed light of my faintest memories, I see my mother and father walking. But already, my current impression of them seeps into the past—I refer to them separately when they were actually one. One unit, one word, one idea: parents.

My mother was waiting for me, replete with hopeful expression, when I got home. "He knew before he even saw me," I said.

During these walks that I just barely remember, my parents converse.

"He had time to decide exactly what he wanted to say. To rehearse it," I said.

Sounds exist, but their speech is beyond my understanding.

"I was terrified," I told her, "of what he would think. Of how to tell him."

How odd to imagine a time before letters, sentences, text, definitions.

"But I didn't have to tell him. Because he already knew."

A time before context, implicatures, and weighty silences.

My mother said nothing. I said nothing in return.

Their sounds were phonemes, part of a system I couldn't comprehend at the time, and though I think I understand it now, I grapple with the universality of meaning. Not between speakers of many tongues, but between speakers of a single language. If it can't cure misunderstanding, why is the system in place at all?

If, when I say, "I don't want to see my father," that is not construed as, "I don't want my father having information about my life," then why do we spend so much time trying to communicate?

Language is necessary. If there were no words—no speech—we would create a new lexicon of symbols. Perhaps one of teeth gnashing or dancing or maybe we'd have a highly evolved telepathy beyond humanity's current capacity for thought. Something would be there for us to learn and manipulate and we would falter or excel because we need it just as badly as we need to be understood. It is our system to try or be tried by and although it sometimes leads to disputes and quarrels, disagreements over what should and can and must or must not be said, language heals more often than it hinders.

I tried to be pragmatic about my parents, tried to put their behavior in context. Maybe I expected too much. After all, my father does lie for a living. His every word is suspect. And my mother—is a mother. She did it to help me, to protect me, to try to save me the hurt. Yet I hurt nonetheless. Possibly more.

I continued to live with her for the six months that followed my visit to my father. During that time, she and I spoke intermittently—we still do—but nothing of significance.

With no one to talk to, nearly shaky from loneliness, I called Patrick. I hoped enough time had passed. I worried the time had been too much. It had already been a year since we'd last seen each other. I was far less cross with him and the distress with my parents changed the distress with Patrick to a familiar, naïve excitement, the sort of feeling a younger me would've called hope.

"Pick up," I told the synthetic ringing as I waited.

"I got your postcard," he said upon answering.

"Good." I let that sit. "I'm home now."

"New York?" he ventured.

"I wish. California."

"Ah. Finished teaching?"

"Teaching didn't quite work out." Eager to pretend that all was well, I changed the subject. "And you? In school, I presume."

"Soon," he said.

"Oh, right. You're off for the summer."

"No." He let the word trail. Something left unsaid.

"Okay," I followed suit.

"I'll be starting in the fall," he admitted.

"You took a year off?"

"I decided to 'explore my options.'"

Never would I have expected him to throw my words in my face in such an offhand fashion.

"Oh," was all I could say. The silence primed us for new levels of discomfort.

"Can I call you back?" Patrick, eternally knocking me off my feet.

"—sure."

He hung up without saying goodbye, the only signal that he was truly still himself.

Shortly thereafter, I capriciously visited UCLA's campus. I missed classes. I missed learning. I mistakenly interpreted that as a desire to spend the rest of my life in academia. That was the first of many mistakes I'd make at UCLA. I'd been on campus for less than an hour when Patrick called me back.

"You have eerily strange timing," I said.

"Have I?"

"Yes. I'm at a school." He knew this meant that I could barely conjure the concept of a classroom without him leaping to mind.

"Which one?"

"UCLA."

"Hmm."

"What? You too good for a state school?"

I spoke to him that day with a confidence I never knew in person. He couldn't see my face, likely envisioned me as completely unchanged. His misconception allowed me to be the person I was when last we'd parted. I missed being her. And she missed being with him.

"Not at all," he said.

"You should visit."

"The school or—"

"—whatever you want."

As if either of us had ever gotten whatever we wanted.

Patrick didn't even attempt a greeting when we saw each other. I assumed there hadn't been anyone else during our year apart, but didn't ask for verification. I was too busy spending my time trying not to blink—not to wink. Luckily, our quality time had never been spent facing each other.

Not long after the rough and tumble, we stared at opposite points of the same ceiling.

"What were you doing at UCLA?" he asked.

"Poking around," I showed him only my profile. "Occasionally, I do miss school."

"Think you'll go there?"

"It's anybody's guess what I'll do. I'd like to be inspired."

"To learn?"

"Does that sound stupid?"

"Actually, it sounds like the exact opposite of stupidity. Literally."

"Yeah." I cast my eyes sideways. "Where will you go?"

"UCLA."

"Shut up," I said.

"I'm serious. They offered me a fellowship. I start in the fall."

I sat up suddenly, my hand covering my eye in the guise of confusion. "Why didn't you tell me?"

"I'm telling you now." I would have avoided him. Could have. I couldn't focus to speak, couldn't talk without crying. "What's wrong?"

"Nothing. Forget it."

"Is this because of your face?"

My blood froze. Any functioning nerves remaining in my face clenched and then released.

"I mean," he went on, "what happened to you? With your—?" He gestured to my right side.

"Nothing! Christ, stop fucking gawking at me!" I kicked the sheets back, then immediately pulled them around me like a shroud. Patrick tugged at them.

"What are you doing?" I remained silent, refusing to face him. "Mere—*Mere*. Would you look at me for a second?" I looked. "Why did you invite me here?"

"I don't know."

"You don't. Really."

"What?" I said.

"You don't need me to help you through whatever the hell happened to you in China?"

I wished I could have pretended he hadn't said it or that I hadn't heard it, but we had passed the point of pretending. "Please don't," I said.

"Don't what? Clearly something fucked up happened to you and it fucked up your face and now you're acting like it's nothing and like I should act like it's nothing when it's obviously upsetting you."

I held my lower lip to my front teeth and exhaled hard through my mouth; the effect was something like an emphatic stutter. "Fuck off, Patrick." My chin dimpled on only one side. I swallowed tremendous breaths of air to stop my chest from heaving. An exit was sorely due. "I don't deserve this," was all I could say, "especially not from you."

I didn't look at him another second. I careened around the room, grabbing a shirt, then pants, then stomping off toward the bathroom where I stayed until I heard the front door open and shut.

In the end, I didn't even apply to UCLA. Not at that point. I was too scared, too intimidated, mostly due to our fight. But I knew what I was missing. I knew I had to go, not as a retreat, but as a next step. Just being on campus had drawn me in. Also, there was the repugnant pull in my nethers. I hated wanting to be near Patrick, hated wanting him to reach out first, hated knowing that it was my turn, but I'm nothing if not self-aware. So I applied to a different school, then transferred. And I let him find me.

We wound up taking the same survey morphology course. He approached me, full of bravado, ready to speak and avoid all mention of our previous meeting.

"I'm surprised to see you here," he said. Knowing full well that I'd mistake his meaning for the school, rather than the class, he clarified. "Phonetics and morphology rarely mix."

"That's true," I played coy. "But I could say the same to you."

"Elective requirement."

"Must be tough," I said. "You're surely bored by all this semantic talk."

"I'm always bored by semantics, but you're avoiding the question."

"You didn't ask a question." Parry.

"It was implied." Dodge.

"Sometimes, I need this things spelled out." Thrust.

"Have you given up phonetics because of your accident?" *Touché.*

"It wasn't an accident," I began.

"I wouldn't know," he lobbed it back at me.

"Look, Patrick," I tried to disguise the pain in my voice. "I haven't forgiven you for what you said when we last spoke, but I know you won't apologize. So I'll offer a compromise. We won't talk about what happened. We won't discuss my condition. You don't ask about it, silently or otherwise. If you're not capable of this, we won't talk at all."

His eyebrows lilted ever so slightly toward his hairline and remained there. "Agreed."

III. Precipice

I hate cake. Its form nauseates me. Hiding in a guileful happiness, it purports a celebratory aura, sometimes being so bold as to boast sprinkles. But as soon as it enters your mouth, it enters your system, and, ultimately, your life, bringing its insidious crystalline glucose in tow.

As a child—such a substance is served to *children*—I dawdled at birthday parties, content to let my ice cream seep slowly into the pores of this sickening "treat" that bore a mendacious name: angel food cake (as if angels preferred to glut themselves on heaps of puffed baggage, sweet enough to make their sinuses water) or the more aptly named devil's food cake, a sticky confection so weighty, it bent the stem of my plastic spoon, the shovel of which sagged under the heft of this playful dessert.

When I deigned an occasion important enough to be worthy of my suffering (my mother's birthday or any holiday wherein I was made to feel guilty because someone had baked), I struggled to choke down each sugary forkful, my eyes wincing from the task. Afterward, I would escape to the sanctity of my room and lie in my bed's center, my body bloated and dimpled from the wreckage.

Idioms like *piece of cake*, words such as *cakewalk*, leave a sour (that is, all too sweet) taste in my mouth. With their original meanings in mind, my visit to my father should be a piece of cake. Visits to one's parents should always be so simple. However, considering my gastronomical preferences, I can truthfully say that my visit will be, every bit and bite, enough cake to choke a Clydesdale.

Swallowing the slick frosting, feeling droplets of icing-sweat clinging to my insides, I stand in his doorway and it is everything I expect it to be. As soon as I see him, the good side of my face goes slack. A chasm lies between us, heat rising from its depths. It blurs my father's form, making his shape less threatening, less like something that might bludgeon the life from me. I need only to cross the room to confront him, but it's like crossing a bridge made of sand. Who's to say it won't collapse under my weight? Better to speak first and use the words as stepping stones.

A thick grasp of fear holds my larynx. I clear my throat ineffectually.

"Eliot?" It's the first word I've heard my father speak aloud in nearly twenty years. Eliot remains silent. I feel his presence as surely as I know there's furniture in the room, but whether he stands beside me or has fallen back, I can't be sure. Such knowledge doesn't better or worsen the task at hand. I become aware of my breath, loud and staggering, and assume my father hears it as well.

"Who's there?" His voice has become raspy in my absence, likely due to age, but I enjoy pretending it's from disuse. Compared to my own voice, my father's appears younger. Though it rasps, the delivery tumbles forth untarnished, its messenger perfectly capable of a full range of round vowels, whether uvular or labial.

I envy my father's labial capabilities. I almost tell him as much, but am instead preoccupied trying to mimic his speech. It's like learning anew; this is my infancy and I emulate his adult language as best I can.

*

My biggest fear in graduate school was being exposed as a dilettante. An undergraduate linguistics major does not a linguist make; on the opposite side of a similar coin, nor does a polyglot. But these are assumptions held by the uninitiated.

My burgeoning interest in graduate studies transformed into the condition I currently suffer from—pedantry—

but long before that, I feared being revealed as the fraud I was. I fretted over potential disrespect, over competitive contemporaries, over cheap digs among colleagues. I spent the first semester at UCLA feeling like a bruised peach on display at a market: often admired, until picked up and viewed from a certain angle.

Was everyone looking at my face? Were they studying my peculiar manner of speech? Probably not. My focus in semantics kept me quiet, let me hide, and since my silence sounded exactly like everyone else's, I pretended I was just like them. We were all so happy to be there, getting paid to study exactly what we wanted. I let everyone believe I loved semantics as much as I'd loved phonetics. I would've tried my hand at phonology, a discipline that might have made me happy if I'd let it, but I couldn't. The idea of a linguistically crippled one-time phonetician studying the theory of the way she used to speak seemed to me too much like a widower kissing the twin of his long dead wife. So I avoided phonetics and phonology and tossed away my hours on silent text, on printed words I knew I'd never hear, like the nine different Farsi words for *paralysis*, or the seven in Arabic, or the four in Chinese. Not a recognizable Roman letter among them—no chance of attempting pronunciation—but even in the Romance and Uralic and Indo-European languages, *paralysis* still ranked high: four words in Portuguese and German, three in Romanian and Croatian, two in

Bulgarian, two more in Estonian. Every language had one and, semantics aside, I was their common link. They were all pronounced the same way in my head, a sound like a yawn or an underwater scream. They sounded like pills do, bubbling backward down my throat, swallowed out of helplessness, a method of surrender. They sounded like second-guessing. They sounded like doubt. They sounded like prohibition. They sounded like me.

I kept researching them.

"Did you know that Bengali has nine words for *paralysis*?" I asked Patrick.

"Yes—"

"And Japanese has five."

"—I know."

Patrick remained a phonetician, consequently attaining a status comparable to sainthood in my eyes, though I've never told him so.

Graduate school was the ideal setting for our relationship. We could admire each other from a distance, take it for granted that we would talk when we wanted to and remain silent when we didn't, and somehow meet somewhere in between.

I don't recall whose idea it was, but during our final year of study, we were living together.

"Patricia."

The name was my commentary on our mounting

domesticity. Patrick was lapping the route between dining room and kitchen, fretting over plates laden with crudités, which wine paired best with what course, and dealing with the general disarray of papers, dog-eared books, and overturned, half-read scholarly journals.

"Patricia," I repeated, sliding my dagger in beneath a sweetness of tone.

"What?" his response was terse and thick with impatience. I knew better than to vocally judge him, so I opted for faux-generosity.

"How can I help?"

"Clean." What a threat.

"What—clean what?"

"Everything," he said. "All of it."

"But some of it is yours."

"So?"

"Your room is full," I reminded him. It's where we'd hidden all the boxes.

"Can't we use your room then?"

His room. My room. Mine, yours, these. Nothing was *ours*, save the event itself: our first dinner party. We'd invited everyone that we knew locally—our professors and classmates—to join us in singing hosannas over a milestone reached: an entire fortnight successfully spent living in the same quarters, a feat achieved easily enough through a carefully plotted system of avoidance. Our separate belongings, boxed and labeled, mapped very specific routes from bathroom to kitchen to each separate bedroom, eventually spilling toward the front door, never the twain to meet. We wouldn't last a year, I would go on to earn my MA—not my PhD—and become a lexicographer who only occasionally ponders sound and mainly lives beholden to meaning; Patrick would forever find that "regrettable," which he'd tell me every few years or so, and then I'd forget about it, which gave him the opportunity to say it again. But neither of us knew that then. We likely would have continued on in our cardboard labyrinth forever had a dining room table not arrived (a gift from Patrick's mother), the accompanying card reading, *Because you need to eat.*

Similar in height and depth to a sarcophagus, the table was lost on Patrick and me, we being chronic culprits of meals consumed at desks between bits of research. The single non-scholarly boon the table offered us—for we almost immediately began amassing a disorderly fortress of phonetic and semantic tomes atop it—was a new place to copulate, an impulse to which we acquiesced only twice: once before the dinner party and once after, amid the soiled place settings and half-remaining candlesticks.

As I stashed the papers and books and paraphernalia into the box the table arrived in, Patrick set the table with the only matching dishes we owned.

"Jesus Christ," he held a knife aloft, inspected its sheen.

"Our flatware is rusting."

"Give me that." I examined the knife and found nothing. "You're seeing things."

"I'm not," he insisted.

"Patrick, the finish on these is supposed to make them look older. That's why we bought them."

His face said he hated our flatware and his eyes said he might hate me, but aloud, he said, "I'm going to work on my article."

Patrick had spent the entire summer revising and elongating an article, written under the tutelage of his advisor, Professor Nesk. Patrick had been planning his segue and his pitch, and was banking on Nesk's connections to hurtle him toward opportunity. A good word from him would ignite Patrick's name in the minds of phoneticians the world over, not to mention the job offers and tenure and security—

But everything hinged on Patrick's continued status as Nesk's assistant. Patrick couldn't conceive of a logical reason why the position would become unavailable to him. Until it was. In the middle of the second course, Nesk began talking about a new project, requiring a new assistant.

"You're going to be thrilled with my choice, Patrick," he said, shaking a fork jovially in Patrick's direction.

"I trust you implicitly," Patrick smiled and turned a pale shade of green. This did not go unnoticed by Nesk.

"I'm sure you'll be happy to have a year to yourself to work on your dissertation." He clapped Patrick's shoulder once to reinforce their camaraderie. I watched the gears move within Patrick's retinas. In that year, he could transfer. He could be at a different school, furthering important projects, sitting first chair on some hypothetical, rewarding student assembly.

Patrick excused himself and walked stoically to the kitchen. I granted him a few moments of privacy before fabricating a possible heavy plate which would warrant my assistance. I crossed the room's threshold and found Patrick leaning, dumbfounded, against the kitchen counter. His entire form trembled. He didn't look up when I entered. I doubt he even knew I was there.

I struggled to overcome my initial shock. Some part of me previously believed that Patrick feared nothing and was impervious to the dread so often known to trickle down other, lesser people's spines. But there he stood, a quaking, quailing child. He drank a fistful—more than four fingers, less than five—of whiskey and finally turned his face to mine. Our bodies quickly followed and soon we were two trembling frames, mine empathetic to his. His arm encircled my waist, a flimsy attempt to maintain support.

"Patrick?"

"Hm." His response arrived more declarative than it should have.

"You'll be fine. Nesk can still recommend you for other projects. He can still be a profitable source of networking for you. You can still go to him for advice." With each successive sentence, I'd hoped his expression would change. His face read as if I'd not said a word. "You'll be fine," I repeated. I said it because I believed it, not because I thought he needed to hear the words, but I should've known better than to attempt to allay Patrick's apprehension over his career. I'd never been able to accept other people's opinions in reference to my future. It was nonsensical to think he'd accept any advice regarding his own.

"No," he said, releasing me. "I won't be *fine.*"

He poured and consumed one last finger of whiskey, then abandoned me in the kitchen. I listened as murmuring became chatter and my faith in Patrick's ability to save both our faces allowed me to slink unceremoniously to the tile floor.

When I re-entered the dining area, Patrick sat alone.

"Where is everyone?"

"Gone."

"I'm sorry. If I'd known—"

"It doesn't matter."

"Patrick. I'm sorry."

"So am I."

"You didn't let me finish. I'm sorry if I spoke out of turn earlier. But I meant what I said."

"You always do." His tone was rich with derision.

"What does that mean?"

"It means that you're so *careful* with everything, down to your jury-rigged pronunciation."

"Excuse me?"

"Not that I'm complaining. That stiff-jawed slackness—or lack thereof—has secured me many a pleasant night's sleep. I'm just saying that when it comes to elocution—"

I was halfway across the room, brandishing my knuckles, by the time Patrick saw me coming. He made the mistake of standing, giving me an easy target. Without hesitation, I punched him directly in the throat.

His speechlessness lasted for the most fleeting of moments; nothing gold can last. "That was my fucking larynx," he wheezed and clutched his neck.

"I know what it was," I said bitterly. "It was *intentional*."

"It was foolish—"

"It was a fucking example of what I have to go through every day. You think nothing of your ease of speech, of your uninhibited points of articulation."

"You're so erudite when you're angry."

"Fuck right off, Patrick. At least you still get to study what you want. You've never had to settle." I stormed past him, aiming for any space he didn't occupy. "Get out of my way."

"I wish you wouldn't be so fucking fragile about

everything," he said.

"Fragile?" I repeated. "Did you honestly just say that to me after your behavior tonight?"

"Apples and oranges."

"No, my dear, it's more like eggs and egos, both of which are incidentally *fragile*. To be fragile. What does that even mean? Let's consider the different definitions."

"*Merde*."

"We might be discussing my tangible form. My brittle bones, the breakability of my skull. That's literal fragility," I rapped my right index and middle fingertips against the side of my head. "But you could also have been speaking metaphorically. My heart, misshapen, bent, and already broken. You needn't worry though, such a metaphor can't kill me. Only *literal* heartbreak would render me incapacitated. Though I doubt you would even be cognizant enough to refer to my heart."

"Now hold on just a second," Patrick began.

"With all due respect, don't you *dare* interrupt me. I've held my tongue on a number of occasions when you weren't even talking about anything noteworthy, much less important." Patrick wearily waved me on. I faltered, then mumbled angrily, "I've lost my place."

"I'll say." I nearly hit him again. "You were going on about my inability to consider your feelings."

"Metaphors! *That's* where I was! You could have been

prevaricating some other figurative take, proposing that just below my skin lays a thin layer of glass."

"Lies."

"I'm being perfectly honest."

"No, I meant *lies*, as opposed to *lays*. You meant *lies*."

"No," I said, "that's only in the past tense. Lie, lay, lain..."

"Yes, but you said, 'it *lays*,' present tense."

"God*dammit*, Patrick, is this really even worthy of discussion? I don't give a damn about the present tense or past tense or any of that right now!"

"But you do!" he said. "And that's why we're talking about this. You care about all the stupid, mundane shit that no one else wants to think about. You care about all of it. And then you accuse me of getting upset over something that actually matters. That's the problem."

"No, Patrick, the problem is that I care about all things and you care about nothing. Not a single fucking thing. Except yourself." I tried to step around him to shut myself in my room, but he put his forearm out to block my path. "Let me go."

"We're not finished discussing this."

"Like hell." I grabbed his wrist in an attempt to gain enough leverage to pass, but he spun out of my grip and pinned my own arm behind me, turning me to face him. "Let me go," I said again.

"Not until you're being rational."

I slapped his face with my free hand, the left, the weaker of the two. "Is that rational enough? Now let *go.*"

Without a word, he spun me back toward the table. He half-dragged, half-carried me to its edge and propped me atop it.

"Patrick," I sounded unwilling. I was still angry. He held my arm behind me and, with his other hand, worked at my skirt and undergarments. I sighed. "Can't you just apologize?"

"No." He unfastened his belt.

"I hate you."

He nodded and, gripping my outer thigh, pulled us together.

Much like my relationship with my father, my interaction with Patrick wasn't always thorns and missiles.

"Meredith," Patrick once murmured to me in a bout of unexpected tenderness. We had just woken from an impromptu afternoon nap and, upon hearing my full, proper name, I lifted my head to see Patrick's earnest eyes waiting for my response.

"Hmm?" My voice was as rumpled as my hair.

"Will you do me a favor?" Accompanying his question was a hand gesture measuring a small plot of air between his thumb and forefinger, indicating the favor's size. I nodded, urging him to continue. "Make me a pot of coffee?"

My tongue writhed against the roof of my mouth while I momentarily averted my eyes. "How many scoops of coffee?" I said, steering my gaze back toward him. I was an herbal tea drinker, so I couldn't begin to fathom the difference between weak and watery or stout and satisfying, nor could I posit a guess for his preference.

"Five scoops of coffee, four cups of water," he told me.

"How do you take it?"

"Black as tar and as soon as it's filtered," he said, shoving me from the bed.

I stood and ambled toward the kitchen, my gait stuttering the entire way. My actions were weighty and bold throughout the coffee's creation. It brought to mind every commercial that pre-dated me, but lived in the public's memory long enough to remain prevalent throughout my childhood. They all seemed to have the same tagline: *Just add water.*

I stood and listened to the machine percolate, monitored its progress as it eked out one, then a couple, then several more cups into the carafe. Initially empty and transparent, the carafe changed as it filled, becoming completely opaque. Through my sleepy wits, the container was as dark as the coffee. The latter had changed the former and the carafe couldn't return to transparency without purging the coffee

Patrick came in, asking, "Is it done?"

I had to force my eyes away from the coffeemaker, had to focus. "I think so," my answer took its time surfacing. Patrick wordlessly thrust a mug toward me. I filled it almost to its brim.

He took the mug from me and drank deeply, greedily. "This is—" he paused for breath. "—*awful.* How long has it been since you last made coffee?"

While I suffered most of Patrick's barbs with, what I viewed as, unwarranted élan, I crumbled immediately at this particular criticism. With no warning, I fell against his chest and howled like a child lost in a supermarket.

"What's wrong?" he asked, terrified of my unprovoked dismay. I shook my head, unwilling to speak. If I thought he had any empathy at all, I might have explained how afraid I was that I would never be able to properly interact with other people, that I feared never being good enough or even adequate because no one ever taught me how to be so. Instead, I boiled it down to its essence.

"I'm afraid I've married my father."

Patrick gasped. "You're married?"

He enjoyed turning my strict adherence to semantics against me. "You know what I meant," I said.

"No, I don't know. I *assume* that you meant I remind you of your father."

"Yes."

"Which makes no sense."

"Why?" I said.

"Because you hate him."

"I don't hate him." Patrick couldn't articulate how contrary I was being, so he instead served me a disbelieving look. "I don't! He's just—difficult."

"How so?"

"The same way you are," I said. "I can't explain it. Little things you do remind me of him. Like the coffee thing. I used to make coffee for him. When he still had a day job."

"Your father had a day job?"

I nodded. "He was an office clerk. It was laughable—not the position itself, but because he's never been good in positions of servitude, nor at being told what to do. So, because I wanted to make his job easier, I volunteered to lessen the burden of his morning routine."

"By making his coffee."

"Yes. Each morning, he made half a pot of coffee which dripped while he showered, then he drank one cup, and took the remainder to work. He even used an old-fashioned thermos, which I admired for its style, practicality, and ease of use. What a fussbudget I was."

"Still are."

"True," I confessed. "My plan was that I would wake early with him, make his coffee, pour one cup for home, stow the rest in his thermos, and put it by the door so he could grab it on his way out."

"Like a tiny assembly line."

"Of sorts, yes." In the beginning, it was precisely what I wanted. He doled out a modicum of gratitude—which I ingested with the zeal and reverence of a Catholic accepting a communion wafer—and we'd go on our ways, that much better for the morning's interaction. I would beam, not just for the opportunity to commingle with everyday adult responsibility, but to be of practical use to my father, whose burden was great and responsibilities many. Besides his paying job, which took more than eight hours from each day, he had to care for my mother and me. And only after all the other things were settled would he sit down to write, and later film, his first project, all of which was luckily set at night. "I admired every last thing he did." I lifted my eyes at the memory, but they sank just as quickly. "He was perfect."

"The problem with perfection," said Patrick, "is its mutability."

I laughed without smiling. "He was my best friend. It's funny how much simpler things are to children. A person is your friend or your enemy. And you're sure they'll never be anything else."

"Who's to say that changes in adulthood?" Patrick asked.

"Our relationship stands to reason against that argument."

Patrick nodded then because he knew that I was right, that we were complicated, and that we'd never be any more or less than that. He was the coffee to my carafe. But even if I could've purged him from my system, I knew I'd never be clear again. We'd never be altogether separate. If I could have explained, I would have told Patrick that that was the biggest reason he reminded me of my father. And that sometimes, it was a comforting evil.

IV. Prognosis

Eliot takes one tentative step out of the room. I flounder, grab his wrist, tug him back. His expression begs for release; I dare not let go.

"You asked me to come here," I say. I exhale like a frustrated dog. "You *can't* leave."

Piteous reassurance surfaces in Eliot's smile, confirming that I'm alone, that his presence grants me nothing. Secure in that knowledge, ready to fight my way out, I relinquish his hand. A sigh within and without; our scene is set.

I am cognizant of being set in my father's crosshairs. My steps fall as anchors would, but I cannot stop here. I'm prepared to cut them loose if necessary.

In order to fill the space with trustworthy sounds, I say,

"It's just me."

See also: It's merely I.

See also: It's me: Mere.

Had my father written this exchange, he would have played the heavy. I would have been cast as the ingénue underdog. Had he directed it, the light would have shown only my good side. My face would never have appeared crooked, my words never imbalanced. The audience would have seen only what he wanted to be true.

My father never invested himself in an unworthy lie.

"Mere." The tenderness of his smile belies our silence and belittles the past. I do not correct his pronunciation. Instead, I look to the walls, which feel on the verge of collapse, then back to his open gaze. My breath appears as half-laughter, half-aspiration—almost *Hello*, on the verge of *How could you?*, very nearly *Help*.

"It's been some time," he tells me. I nod stiffly, timidly. "Would you like to sit?"

"No." The furniture seems menacing as a promise. "Thank you."

"Would you like anything to drink?" I shake my head guiltily, as if I should have arrived thirsty. "Surely you'll have something—wine?"

My head continues shaking.

"Tea?"

Thank you, no.

"Water?"

Here, I hold up my hand. I'm not interested in breaking bread or water or wine or anything resembling pleasantries. His questions cease.

"I heard," my voice ambles, "that you're...sick."

"Sick?" my father seems genuinely surprised. "No. I had a cold earlier this month, but I've since recovered."

"I didn't mean it that way, Dad." There's a word: *Dad.* I hadn't said it in decades, not in reference to him. After our separation, he had ceased being my Dad, and had since been *my father.* The terms, up to this point, had been mutually exclusive in my mind. "I meant—I read about you. In the *Times.*"

"Oh," he chuckles lightly. "You can't believe what they put in those papers."

"It was online." Always the stickler. Mean what you say. Say what you mean.

"Even worse. Automatic publishing. I don't think they even have proofreaders for those things."

I release a slight nod. "Dad," I use the word here as a leverage tool, one of persuasion, "Eliot called me."

"Did he?"

"Yes." His lightness of tone shakes me, but I press on. "Yes, he did. He said you needed my help."

"Eliot—is a good friend. Always looking out for me." He smiles absently. "Why, I've known him since you were..."

Here he pauses and along with him, my heart. Has he forgotten my age? And if so, is it because of his illness or because of my absence? He holds up a hand, close to his knee, "...since you were this high."

"I think I was a little taller at that point," I say to mask my relief.

"Maybe," he admits.

"So," I persist, "it's not true?" I want definitive proof. "You're all right?"

"I'm fine." So often, *I'm fine* stands in place of *Please leave.* So often, *I'm fine* actually means *I need help.* However, to punctuate his meaning, my father's temples grow more defined and his jaw more square, all the signs of a firmly closed mouth, the universal symbol of a person who refuses to speak.

"You can tell me—if you need anything," I say.

"I don't. Need anything."

"Dad."

"Yes?"

Yes. Affirmative. Questioning. He does not choose to say, "What?" It's all politeness here.

"What you have—your illness. It's serious." He does not gesture. He only looks to the corner of the room that lies behind my left shoulder. Then back. "You should see someone. I mean, have you?"

"I see people all the time."

And what is this? A joke? Levity in the guise of misunderstanding?

"I'm sure you do, Dad." Dammit. Does it always have to be tit for tat? Why can't I just let silence answer for me? "I'm sure you see lots of people. But that's not what I meant." He knows what I meant.

"No—" he says. Then nothing. We watch each other as if waiting for our turns to speak, pretending that this verbal volleying is no more than a game at which we've both already given up.

I can think of nothing more to say. I search his face for any signs of weakness and find none. Instead, I find an entrance. I experience a connection where previously, there had been only polarity. I am sick with stubborn pride and see that sickness aimed back at me. I am every bit my father's daughter. Looking at him now, I feel closer to him than I have in years. I am him; I am *not* him. He is *me*, crouched on a cot in China, determined to outlive his predicament. How futile my attempts at estrangement seem, my yearning for singledom, my misguided wish to be an island. I can neither remove his impression nor his influence from my genes. I didn't need him, didn't want to admit to needing anyone. He didn't—*doesn't*—need me. He never did.

That, but little else, I can respect about him. That, but little else, I understand.

"Dad."

"Mm?"

"I'm sorry."

"Sorry?" his response appears slowly. I back out of the room, watching my father watching me go.

I confer with Eliot. "You have my number, if you need me."

"Yes," he says.

"I'm sorry I couldn't do more."

Eliot looks not at me, but back toward the room where my father still stands. "You tried."

After leaving, I call the only person who might understand my simultaneous desires to turn around and to run away. He picks up almost immediately.

"Did you see him?" Patrick, the incapable greeter.

"Yes—it hurt. Not that I thought it wouldn't."

"Do you want to talk about it?" he asks.

"Of course not," I admit.

"Of course not," he repeats.

"I'm not sure what I expected. I went in having nothing prepared to say."

"It wasn't a conference," he says.

"But I should've said more. Done more."

"Such as? Dredged up the past? Would that have helped?"

"Considering our track record, it might've made things

worse. I wonder how much of it he remembers. Even if he were well— But isn't that what I have you for? As a relic of years gone by?"

"When you say it like that," he says, "it might be better to ask why I stay."

Two questions we both avoid. Our mutual fear of sentimentality allows me to change the subject. "Listen, what are you doing now?"

"Very little, why?"

Not wanting to be by myself, I create an excuse for minimal contact, an activity wherein we could share the same space, but not have to interact. "Do you want to go to the theatre? I have season tickets."

A violin concerto fills the cab. All the sound is unwarranted, unexpected, and exactly what I require from the moment. The music demands a reverent silence, leaving me to mentally wander. I glance furtively at Patrick, guiltily wishing that he—and we—were different. Easier to read, more willing to bend, to bond. Knowing better, I wish for a catalyst, some arbitrary force to remove the guesswork from my decisions.

The violins sing on, complementary in their trilling, headed toward crescendo. There is beauty in their wordlessness.

I catch a chill, whether caused by the setting or my mood, I can't be sure, but I inadvertently reach for my collar to tighten a scarf I'm not wearing. A throwback to New York: when I close my eyes, I'm as good as there.

Someday, someday soon, my father will believe I live there. He'll believe me back to college. His memories will make me over, over and over again. I'll be the person I was before our split, the phonetician I was before my face. I'll still be with Patrick, but then I'll be without, no wiser for our parting since we will have never been. I'll be an almost artist. I'll be a silent daughter, a child before speech, with only my parents' memories as proof I lived at all. How many of those days will my father remember? How many movie premieres, press conferences, ceremonies, feasts?

He'll remember as many as he'll forget.

Patrick and I sit together, knuckles abutting, but exist leagues apart. One theatergoing dinner date is exchangeable for another.

We reach La Jolla, where he waves away my offer to pay the fare. It was less generosity on my part and more hesitance to leave the confines of the cab. I preferred to soldier on in that silence, wanted its confident protection to envelop me always, to lull me into a womblike haze. But I emerge too soon, pushed into the outside, with no chance of being reborn.

Acknowledgments

My gratitude is owed to the following individuals: Carolina Barerra-Tobón, for helping me establish a solid base in linguistics; Neal Bruss, for assigning *The Biography of the English Language* and explaining in short order why jargon must be used sparingly; Sandy McClintock, for encouraging me because she knew things that I didn't; Randolph Pfaff, for always being willing to read everything I write, no matter the number of iterations he's previously read; Shannon Derby, for her acute insight into second and third drafts; Cynthia Reeser for her diligence, patience, and flexibility, and Meredith Conti, for signing her e-mails in a way that made me want to name a character after an adjective.

About the Author

Carissa Halston's debut novel, *A Girl Named Charlie Lester*, was honorably mentioned in the 2008 New York Book Festival. Her short fiction has appeared or is forthcoming in *TRNSFR*, *Consequence*, *The Collagist*, and *The Massachusetts Review*. She has received scholarships for her fiction from Wesleyan Writers Conference and University of Massachusetts Boston. She currently lives in Boston where she edits a literary journal called *apt*, hosts a reading series called Literary Firsts, and is at work on a novel called *Conjoined States*.

CPSIA information can be obtained at www.ICGtesting.com
Printed in the USA
BVOW010116150812

297914BV00001B/18/P